BORROWED BLACK

A Labrador Fantasy

Copyright © 1988 Ellen Bryan Obed — text
Jan Mogensen — illustrations
A Breakwater Books Original Publication.

Canadian Cataloguing in Publication Data

Obed, Ellen Bryan, 1944-
  Borrowed Black

    ISBN 0-920911-14-5

I. Mogensen, Jan   II. Title

PS8579.B42B67 1988   jC813'.54   C88-098559-3
PZ7.O23Bo 1988

BORROWED BLACK

A Labrador Fantasy

Ellen Bryan Obed
illustrated by Jan Mogensen

BREAKWATER

No one who belongs to the Labrador
Knows where Borrowed Black lived before
He came to stay on the tall, dark shore
On the wildest tickle of Labrador.

Some say he came like a wolf through the snow;
Some say he came like a seal on a floe;
Some say he came like a jaeger in flight;
Some say he came like fog in the night.

He borrowed the ugliest rock he could find
Where the wind like a husky howled and whined,
Where the sea would come hissing and slapping inside
And urchins and eels floated in on the tide.

He borrowed boards from boats he had found —
Some that were floating, some that had drowned.
Then he built a shack for the wickedest weather
And caught 200 creatures to hold it together.

He stayed there and no one went to his shack,
For Borrowed Black borrowed and never gave back.
He borrowed his hands from the claws of a bear.
A patch of brown seaweed he borrowed for hair.

His eyes were a wolf's, and he borrowed to hear —
Two empty seashells — one for each ear.
He borrowed a beak from a gull for a nose.
He cut off the sails of schooners for clothes.

He walked on seal flippers; they were his feet.
He borrowed two whale's teeth so he could eat.
He had a borrowing wind for a heart
That held him together each small borrowed part.

But some of that wind he often would use
To borrow whenever, whatever he'd choose.
That wind he kept on the windowsill
In a fishskin sack so it would not spill.

One night Borrowed Black went out with his sack
And borrowed the moon, but on his way back

The moon broke in pieces — a billion and four,

So he buried them deep off the Labrador.

And Borrowed Black greedily grinned with pleasure
To think he had borrowed so tremendous a treasure.

Now the night had nothing of silver to hold;
The winds were crying; the rocks were cold.
The air was thick and dark and chill
And no one could tell where the sea met the hill.

The young rabbits shivered waiting for day;
The owls were hungry but couldn't find prey.
The partridge and fox in the woods nearby
Looked long and frightened to the empty sky.

Only the fishermen in a nearby town
Knew who had taken the silver moon down,
But they dared not go to the ugly shack
To ask for the moon from Borrowed Black.

And Borrowed Black dreamt with an ocean snore
Of silver as he sat on a stump by his door
As seventeen seasons of night went by
With not a piece of moon in the sky.

Then one night from the north in a gale
Came the boat that was built in the back of a whale,

With a tail for its sail and a fifty-foot spout
That a sculpin would climb with his spy to look out.

Now the sculpin had seen some seasons before
The moon taken down and buried off-shore.
He had seen through the night Borrowed Black go,
So he told Cabbage Captain who was steering below.

For seventeen seasons along Labrador
They had searched for Borrowed Black's shack on the shore.

They came to a tickle this night in the storm
With Stove-Pipe Beard coughing to keep the boat warm.
Mousie Mate chattered, "There's something on shore;
I hear through the gale a terrible snore!"

Now the sculpin could see a small shack through the weather
That 200 creatures held tightly together.
Chewing on cabbage and trying to steer,
Cabbage Captain called, "Anchor! Borrowed Black must live here!"

Up got Sinky Sailor who was happy and round,
Who always was laughing without making a sound.
He jumped into the tickle with rope in his hand
To sit on the bottom while the crew got to land.

The Curious Crew were nine shapes and sizes;
They couldn't stop looking about for surprises.
They looked over and under and in what they passed;
They went everywhere mumbling and everywhere fast.

They paddled to shore on an old knotted log;
Mousie Mate sat in front, peering into the fog.

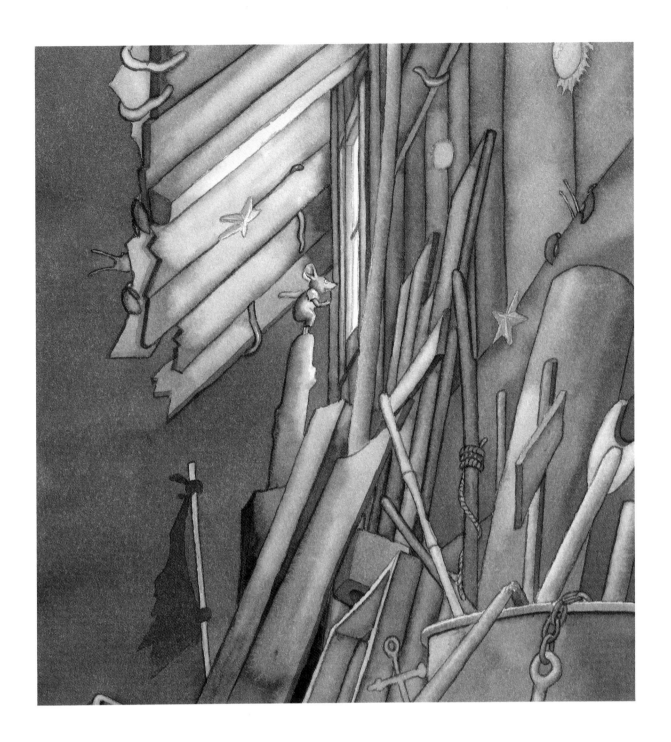

When they reached the shore, Mousie Mate crept
Up to the shack where Borrowed Black slept,
But the Curious Crew were left far behind
Looking over and under the things they could find.

When he looked to the windowsill, Mousie Mate grinned,
For there was the sack with the borrowing wind,
But Borrowed Black sat on his stump by the door
Still dreaming of silver with an ocean snore.

In Mousie Mate tiptoed and picked up the sack
But he squeaked as he scurried out through the crack.

Borrowed Black heard and opened one eye
To see Mousie Mate with the sack going by.

He cried, "That wind is part of my heart!
If you don't give it back, I'll soon fall apart!"

He chased Mousie Mate down the rocks in the fog;
Mousie Mate squeaked as he jumped to the log.
"Tell us, Borrowed Black, where the moon pieces lie.
You'll not have your wind 'til the moon's in the sky!"

*So Borrowed Black boarded and pointed the way
Far off and deep down where the moon pieces lay.*

Mousie Mate let the wind from its sack
To gather the pieces of moon to take back.
It tried to mend the moon with its blow
But the moon would break when the wind let go.

So the wind more thoughtful of night and its kin
Would not return to the sack again.
It stayed in the moon, and as night turned to day...

Borrowed Black fell apart, and each part blew away.

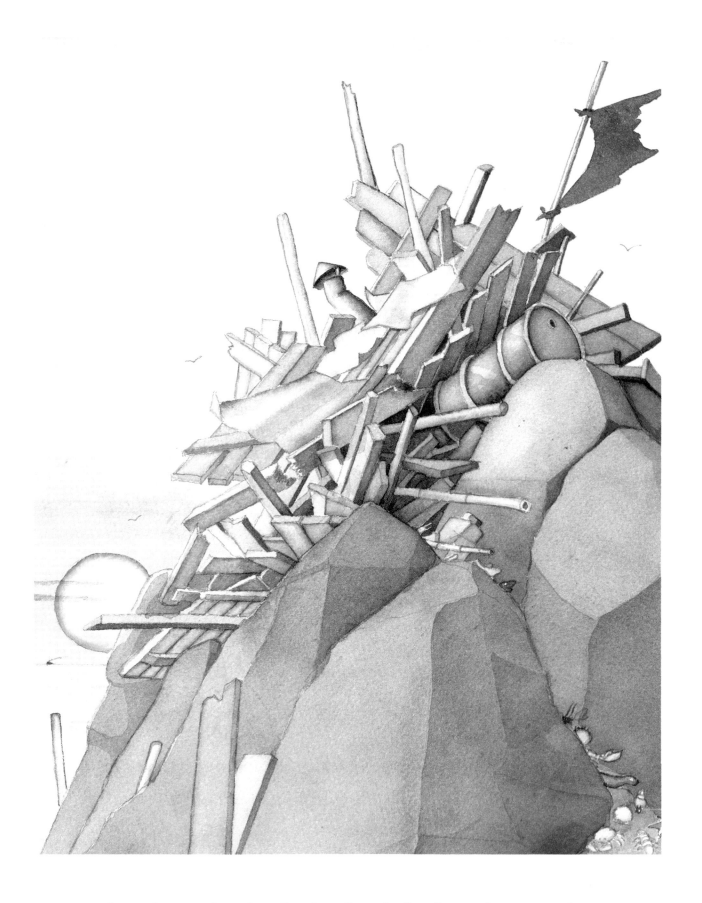

Then his ugly shack shook 'til the boards were free
And the 200 creatures went back to the sea.

To this very night on the Labrador
When you stand and watch from the tall, dark shore,
You can see the cracks in the moon round and high
And the silver it left on its way to the sky.

And the fishermen say if you follow the trail,
You'll come to the boat in the back of the whale.

ac